The Tongue-cut Sparrow

retold by MOMOKO ISHII · illustrated by SUEKICHI AKABA
translated from the Japanese by KATHERINE PATERSON

LODESTAR BOOKS   E. P. DUTTON   NEW YORK

Once, long long ago,
there lived an old man and an old woman.

Because they had no children, the old man adopted a little sparrow that he cared for very, very lovingly.

One day, while the old man had gone to the forest
to gather firewood, the old woman was in the yard doing
her laundry. Suddenly the sparrow, playing above her in
the tree, spied the starch the old woman had boiled, and
swooped down and drank it all up. When she realized what
the sparrow had done, the old woman blazed with fury.
"You good-for-nothing bird! I'll show you!" she cried. And
grabbing up her scissors, *chokin*—she snipped the sparrow's
tongue.

Crying *chun chun*, the poor little sparrow fled toward the
mountains.

When the old man returned later that day, no little sparrow flew out to greet him. "Grandma, oh Grandma," called the old man, "where is my sparrow?"

The old woman replied, "Sparrow? If it's the sparrow you mean, that worthless bird drank up all my starch, so I snipped its tongue. Last I saw, it was flying right out of here, crying *chun chun* all the way home."

"What a cruel thing to do!" cried the old man. "I must go at once to make apologies to the sparrow." So saying, the old man, cane in hand, started for the mountains.

> Sparrow, oh sparrow,
> Oh where is the home of the sparrow,
> *Chun chun*?

he called as he walked.

When he had gone a little way, he came to a place where there was a man bathing oxen. The old man raised his voice and called out, "Ox washer, ox washer, do you know the home of the tongue-cut sparrow?"

And the ox washer answered, "Oh, the home of the tongue-cut sparrow, is it? Well, if you want to know that, you must help me wash these oxen."

So the old man scrubbed the oxen with all his might until finally, *binga binga*, the oxen began to gleam. When he saw this, the ox washer was delighted. "Oh, you wash well! So—go straight up this path. There you will see a man washing horses. Ask him about the home of the tongue-cut sparrow," he said.

Thereupon, the old man once more took up his cane, and as he headed into the mountains, he called:

> Sparrow, oh sparrow,
> Oh where is the home of the sparrow,
> *Chun chun*?

Soon he came to the place where a man was bathing horses. The old man raised his voice and called, "Horse washer, horse washer, where is the home of the tongue-cut sparrow?"

And the horse washer replied, "Oh, the tongue-cut sparrow, is it? If you want to know that, you must help me wash these horses."

Again the old man scrubbed with all his might until finally, *binga binga,* all the horses shone. When he saw this, the horse washer was overjoyed. "Oh, you wash well! So— go straight up this path. Soon you will come to a great bamboo grove. In the middle of the grove is the home of the tongue-cut sparrow. Your sparrow will be wearing a red apron and weaving on a loom," the man told him.

Once again the old man took up his cane, calling as he went:

> Sparrow, oh sparrow,
> Oh where is the home of the sparrow,
> *Chun chun*?

At length, he came to the great bamboo grove, where many sparrows were flying about. And there, in the middle of the grove, was a splendid house. And in the weaving room of the house sat the tongue-cut sparrow, wearing a red apron and weaving away at the loom.

When the sparrow heard the old man's voice, it came rushing out of the house. "Dear old Grandfather, welcome to my humble house," it said.

The old man replied, "When I heard that my old woman had snipped your tongue, I had to come to present my apologies."

"No, no," the sparrow said, "there is nothing to apologize for. I am only too happy to see you again."

Then it gathered all the other sparrows, and together they escorted the old man into the parlor of the house. They put before him the whitest rice and tastiest fish and all kinds of elegant dishes. "Please, please," they urged him, "eat, eat."

The old man feasted until he was stuffed, after which the sparrows entertained him with music and dancing. And then he spent the night in the home of the tongue-cut sparrow.

Early the next morning when the old man was about to leave, the sparrows said, "We'd like to give you a memento of your visit to take home with you."

Whereupon four servants appeared from inside the house carrying two wicker baskets, one large and the other small. "Please," they said, "choose one—either the big one or the little one. It doesn't matter which. But Grandfather, until you reach your own home, you must not take off the lid."

At this the old man said, "I'm an old fellow, so I'd better take the small one." And hoisting the small basket onto his back, he said good-bye to the sparrows.

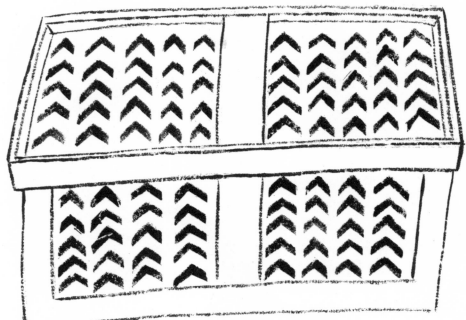
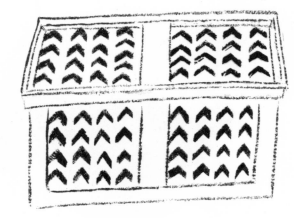

When the old man got home, he and the old woman opened the basket and looked in, and what do you think they saw? Coral treasures great and small, gold and silver, and all kinds of precious things, pouring out of the basket.

Well—the more she saw, the greedier the old woman became.

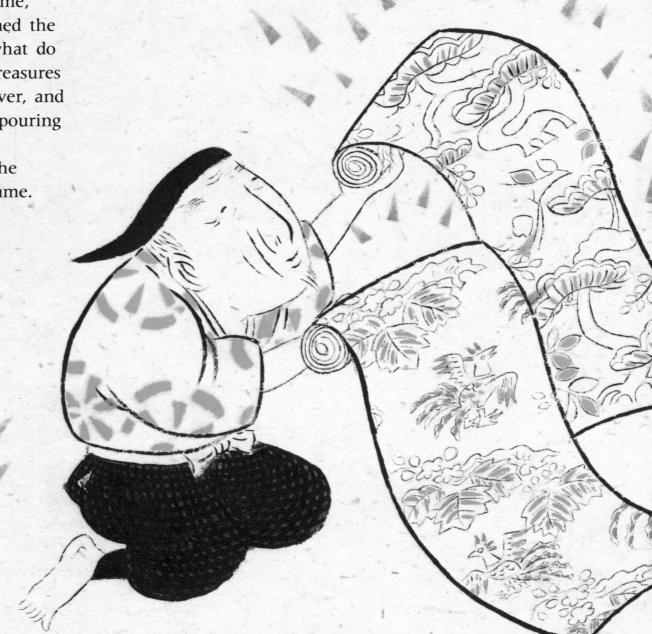

She got directions from the old man, pulled on her leggings, grabbed her cane, and headed for the mountains as fast as she could go.

> Sparrow, oh sparrow,
> Oh where is the home of the sparrow,
> *Chun chun*?

she bellowed as she went.

When she had gone a little way, she came to the place where the man was bathing oxen.

"Hey you! Scrubbing the cows!" she bawled. "Where's the house of the tongue-cut sparrow?"

"Huh? The tongue-cut sparrow's house, you say?" said the ox washer. "If you want to know that, help me wash these oxen."

"Right," the old woman answered. And *kocho kocho,* she gave the dirty oxen a lick here and a lick there. "Done. Now—where's that tongue-cut sparrow?" she demanded.

So he told her that a little further on she would see a man bathing horses, and she should ask him the way.

The old woman took the path as the ox washer had directed, and by and by she came upon the man who was bathing horses.

"Hey you! Scrubbing the horses!" she bawled. "Where's the house of the tongue-cut sparrow?"

At this place, too, she was told that she must help wash the horses. So *gosho gosho*, she gave the dirty horses a splash here and a splash there, and got directions to the next path.

Hurrying on her way, she soon came to the great bamboo grove. Many sparrows were flying about, and there in the house in the middle of the grove sat the tongue-cut sparrow in its red apron, weaving away at the loom.

"Hey you in there! It's Granny," bawled the old woman, "come to see the tongue-cut sparrow!"

"Ah, it's the worthy Grandmother. Dear Grandmother, with what honorable business have you made your way hither?" the sparrow asked.

"You heard me! I've come to see the tongue-cut sparrow."

At this, the tongue-cut sparrow came out of its house and, together with the other sparrows, ushered the old woman inside.

However, the room that they escorted the old woman into was not the parlor but the kitchen. And the food they put before her was millet gruel and grass soup.

The old woman shoved everything right down. "Done," she said. "I've got to go home now. It's getting dark and my old man is waiting. So—what about my present?"

"Well," said the sparrows. "We shall give you one. But Grandmother, we warn you that you must not open the lid until you are all the way home." So saying, the servants brought out two wicker baskets, just as the old man had described.

"I'm a tough old granny," the old woman said, "so I'll take the big one." And hoisting the large basket onto her back, she left the sparrow's house in high spirits.

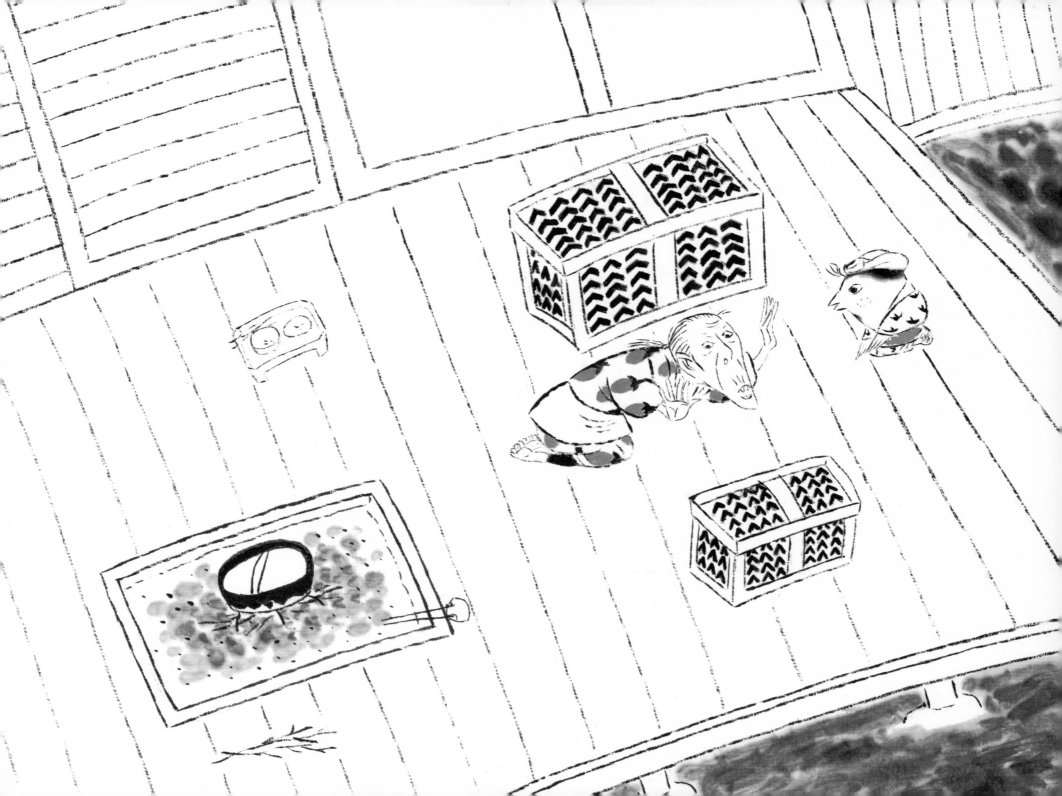

But the basket was very, very heavy, and the old woman had not gone far before she was totally exhausted. She sat down on the root of a tree to rest, and as she rested, she began to think. There was no question, the reason the basket was so heavy was that it was loaded with treasures. As she thought about this, the old woman couldn't stand to wait another minute. She had to see what was in the basket. So—she loosened the rope, lifted the lid, and peeped inside.

A glint of something dusky, a gleam of something dark was all that could be seen.

"A bar of silver! A teapot of gold!" cried the old woman.

Then—*suru suru*—slowly the bar of silver began to rise until it coiled itself around the old woman's arm. A huge snake! And—*yota yota*—the golden teapot came wobbling up until *futt,* it blew a great puff right into the old woman's face. A huge, huge toad!

"*Hi-yaaaa!* The goblins have got me!" the old woman bellowed. Then, jumping to her feet, she ran and ran and ran all the way home, and barely, just barely escaped with her life.

And from that time on, the old woman was cured of greediness, so they say.

Note to the Reader

The story of the kind old man and his greedy wife appears in folktales from all over the world. A Japanese variation on this theme is the story of the tongue-cut sparrow. The reteller, the illustrator, and the translator want you to have fun reading their version of this familiar tale. The Japanese language has a lot of onomatopoeic words, and some of them are retained to add flavor to the English translation.

binga binga (beengah beengah) When something is sparkling clean, it seems to go *binga binga*. Smile when you say these words, and they will twinkle.

chokin (choh-keen) Since this is the sound scissors make in snipping, the two syllables must be spoken very quickly and sharply. Try a little accent on the second syllable.

chun chun (choon choon) This is the sound of a sparrow's chirping.

futt (hoot) This should sound like an explosive puff of hot breath. Try putting a little *f* into your puff, but don't let your teeth touch your bottom lip.

gosho gosho (gohshoh gohshoh) These words are meant to sound like a careless sloshing of water rather than careful scrubbing; so say them fast.

hi-yaaaa (he-yaaaah) No one who's seen a martial arts movie needs help with this exclamation.

kocho kocho (kohchoh kohchoh) These words should be said very fast, to indicate how carelessly and how hurriedly the old woman slapped a bit of water on the dirty oxen.

suru suru (sooroo sooroo) This slippery, sliding sound doesn't need an explanation. It should be said softly and quickly.

yota yota (yohtah yohtah) This is an awkward, wobbling sound. Take it slowly, but don't drag out the vowels.

Shita-kiri Suzume—The Tongue-cut Sparrow
Text copyright © 1982 Momoko Ishii
Illustrations copyright © 1982 Suekichi Akaba
English translation copyright © 1987 by Katherine Paterson

All rights reserved.

Originally published in Japan 1982 by Fukuinkan Shoten, Publishers Inc., Tokyo
First published in the United States 1987 by E. P. Dutton,
2 Park Avenue, New York, N.Y. 10016, a division of NAL Penguin Inc.
Published simultaneously in Canada by Fitzhenry & Whiteside Limited, Toronto

Printed in Japan   COBE   ISBN: 0-525-67199-4   10 9 8 7 6 5 4 3 2 1

Library of Congress Cataloging-in-Publication Data

Ishii, Momoko, date   The tongue-cut sparrow.

Translation of: Shita-kiri suzume.
Summary: A kind old man and his greedy wife pay separate visits to the tongue-cut sparrow and receive as gifts just what they deserve.
[1. Folklore—Japan. 2. Sparrows—Folklore]
I. Akaba, Suekichi, ill.   II. Shita-kiri suzume.
III. Title.
PZ8.1.I743To 1987   398.2'4528883   [E] 86-29314
ISBN 0-525-67199-4

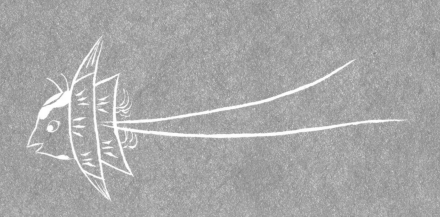